AUNT MABEL'S
TABLE

written by Bob Hartman
pictures by Richard Max Kolding

STANDARD
PUBLISHING
Cincinnati, Ohio

The Standard Publishing Company, Cincinnati, Ohio
A division of Standex International Corporation
© 1994 by The Standard Publishing Company
All rights reserved.
Printed in the United States of America.
01 00 99 98 97 96 95 94   5 4 3 2 1

Library of Congress Catalog Card Number 94-2766
ISBN 8-7847-0178-4
Cataloging-in-Publication data available

Edited by Diane Stortz
Designed by Coleen Davis

CONTENTS

Five Cans

There were five cans

on Aunt Mabel's table.

One for Aunt Mabel.

One for my cousin Sue.

One for Uncle Joe.

One for my cousin Tom.

And one for me, Alexander.

Yes, there were five cans

on Aunt Mabel's table.

And not one of them had a label.

"I got them
on sale
at the supermarket!"
said Aunt Mabel.
"This is a game we play,"
whispered Sue.
"You have to eat
whatever is in your can,"
sighed Uncle Joe.
"I got dog food last time,"
laughed Tom.
I want to go home,
I thought.

6

And then I remembered
what my mother had said:
"Your Aunt Mabel
is a little funny.
Just try to be polite."

A Can for Aunt Mabel

There were five cans

on Aunt Mabel's table.

"I am the oldest,"

said Aunt Mabel.

"So I get to go first."

Aunt Mabel picked up

the biggest can.

She looked at its top

and at its bottom.

She looked all around its sides.

Then she held it to her ear

and shook it.

Everybody listened.

"Sounds like

sweet yellow peaches,"

guessed Aunt Mabel.

"Sounds like

round red tomatoes,"

guessed Sue.

"Sounds like

tiny white potatoes,"

guessed Uncle Joe.

"The kind that make me sneeze."

"Sounds like

dog food," guessed Tom.

"I don't know," I said.

"It just sounds all splashy and splooshy to me."

Aunt Mabel banged the can
on the kitchen counter.
She pulled a can opener
out of a drawer.
She cranked off the lid
in a flash.

Then she held the can

in the air and smiled.

"Peaches!" she said.

"I love peaches!"

A Can for Sue

There were four cans

on Aunt Mabel's table.

My cousin Sue took the smallest.

She looked at its top

and at its bottom.

She looked all around its sides.

Then she held it to her ear

and shook it.

Everybody listened.

"Sounds like soft flaky tuna,"
guessed Aunt Mabel.

"Or yummy pink salmon,"
guessed Sue.

"Sounds like that lumpy
meat spread," guessed Uncle Joe.

"The kind that makes me burp."

"Sounds like dog food,"
teased Tom.

"I don't know," I said. "It just
sounds all soft and squishy
to me."

Sue placed the can

on the counter

and opened it carefully.

She turned around

with the can in her hands

and an awful look

on her face.

"Mushrooms," she moaned.

"I hate mushrooms!"

A Can for Uncle Joe

There were three cans

on Aunt Mabel's table.

They were all about

the same size now.

Uncle Joe sighed

and took the one

in the middle.

He looked at its top

and at its bottom.

He looked all around its sides.

Then he held it to his ear

and shook it.

Everybody listened.

"Sounds like

long stringy beans,"

guessed Aunt Mabel.

"Sounds like

creamed corn," guessed Sue.

"Sounds like

those kidney beans

you always buy,"

guessed Uncle Joe.

"The kind that make me itch."

"Sounds like

dog food," guessed Tom.

"Sounds like . . . peas?"

I said with a shrug.

I was trying to be polite.

Uncle Joe put the can

on the counter.

But he had trouble opening it.

"Hurry!" shouted Aunt Mabel.

"This is so exciting!"

At last,

Uncle Joe got the lid off.

He turned around

and sighed.

"Kidney beans," he said.

"I itch already."

A Can for Tom

There were two cans

on Aunt Mabel's table.

Tom picked up

the one without a dent.

He looked at its top

and at its bottom.

He looked all around its sides.

Then he held it to his ear

and shook it.

Everybody listened.

"Sounds like

pork and beans,"

guessed Aunt Mabel.

"Sounds like

cranberry sauce," guessed Sue.

"Sounds like

thick soup," guessed Uncle Joe.

"The kind you add water to."

"It had better not be

dog food," said Tom.

"Sounds like spaghetti!"

I guessed.

I was catching on.

29

Tom opened the can
as quickly as he could,
just to get it over with.
But before
he could turn around,
I stuck my head
over his shoulder
and peeked.

"I was right!" I shouted.

"It *is* spaghetti!"

"I hate spaghetti,"

said Tom.

One Can Left

There was one can

left on Aunt Mabel's table.

I swallowed hard

and picked it up.

If I was going to be polite,

I would have to eat

whatever was in it.

I looked at its top
and at its bottom.
I looked all around
its dented sides.

Then I held it
to my ear
and shook it.
It made no sound
at all.

For the first time,

Aunt Mabel looked serious.

"It could very well

be dog food," she guessed.

"Or cat food," guessed Sue.

"Probably

beef and liver flavor,"

guessed Uncle Joe.

"The kind that smells so bad."

"Bow-wow," barked Tom.

I said nothing.

I put the can on the counter.

I stuck the sharp bit

of the can opener

into the top

and started to turn

the handle.

I turned the handle ten times.
Then I carefully pulled
up the lid of the can.

What I saw inside

was brown

and thick

and gooey.

It was

a whole can

of chocolate

pudding!

Time to Be Polite

There were five of us

at Aunt Mabel's table.

Aunt Mabel stuck a big spoon
into her bowl of peaches.
"Thank you for coming
to dinner," she said to me.

My cousin Sue
looked at her plate
of mushrooms
and said nothing.

My Uncle Joe stared

at his dish of kidney beans

and started scratching.

My older cousin Tom

asked to leave the room.

But I remembered what my mother
had told me.

"Thank you for having me," I said.

Then I stuck

a big spoon

into my chocolate pudding

and ate it all up.

I was very polite!